ISBN 978-1-84135-786-7

Adapted by Jane Carruth
Illustrated by Rene Cloke

This edition first published 2010

Published by Award Publications Limited,
The Old Riding School, The Welbeck Estate,
Worksop, Nottinghamshire, S80 3LR

10 1

Printed in China

The Wind in the Willows

Mr Toad
in Trouble

From Kenneth Grahame's
Classic Stories

Award Publications Limited

Early one summer morning, Ratty
and Mole set about painting and
varnishing their boat.

Mole worked as hard as Ratty, but he
couldn't help wishing they had eaten a little
something before they had started.

"I suppose we can go in soon for
breakfast," Mole said at last. "There's not
much left to do now."

"Of course we can," smiled Ratty.

Once they had finished, Ratty set about preparing breakfast, and they were in the little parlour enjoying their boiled eggs when there was a loud knock at the door.

"Would you see who it is, Mole?" asked Ratty.

Mole ran to the door and opened it.

"Goodness me! It's you, Mr Badger," he gasped. "Do come in!"

Badger looked very worried as he told Ratty and Mole the news. "Foolish Mr Toad's new motor car arrives today. We must hurry to Toad Hall at once to save him from doing himself a mischief in it."

The three friends set off straight away.

When they reached Toad Hall, they saw that they were just in time. There was Toad, wearing goggles and a smart motoring outfit, about to climb into his shiny new car.

"Hello, you fellows!" Toad called out cheerfully, "You're just in time to come for a jolly—"

Before he could finish, Ratty and Mole grabbed a firm hold of him.

As Toad struggled and kicked in an effort to break free, Badger addressed the delivery man. "You may take the car back, my good man," said Badger, in a very lordly manner. "Mr Toad will not be requiring it after all."

Then, as the car drove away, Badger ordered his friends to take Toad into the house and stay with him.

Toad was spluttering with fury as
Ratty and Mole began pulling off his new
motoring clothes.

And then Mr Badger appeared.

"I'm ashamed of you, Toad," he began
in a stern voice. "I've heard that you were
boasting that you would be the Terror of
the Highway in your motor car!"

At this, Toad struggled more furiously
than ever and it took Ratty and Mole all
their strength to hold him down.

When he could wriggle no more, he said in a feeble voice, "I know that I was wrong. Do please let me go now."

But no sooner was he on his feet than he shouted, "Ha! I'll do whatever I please, you meddling oafs!"

This was too much for Mr Badger. He gave Toad a stern look and then led him off to the drawing room for a sound talking to.

Ratty and Mole waited anxiously for Badger's return. When at last he came back with Toad he looked very serious indeed.

"Toad is quite impossible," Badger told them. "He refuses to say he is sorry, and he won't promise to stay away from fast motor cars in future."

"That's right I won't!" Toad shouted.

"Take him upstairs," Badger ordered. "And make sure that he doesn't leave his room until he comes to his senses."

"It's for your own good, Toady," Ratty said, as Toad kicked and struggled all the way up to his room. "We'll take turns to watch over you."

Even as Ratty was speaking, Toad began arranging the bedroom chairs to look like a motor car. Then he climbed in and began making loud motor car noises.

"I'm afraid it really is bad this time," Ratty whispered. "We'll all just have to stay here at Toad Hall and look after him."

Toad paid no attention to his friends. He just went on pretending to be a racing driver.

After a few days in his room Toad asked
Ratty to come and see him.

"My dear old friend," Toad began in a
feeble whisper, "I am terribly ill. Sleep is
impossible and my poor head throbs..."

"Poor Toady!" Ratty murmured.

"Fetch me a doctor from the village,"
Toad begged. "It may already be too late,
but I need help right away."

Ratty thought that Toad
did not look so very poorly,
but he felt sorry for his
friend, so he agreed to go.

Toad knew that Mole
and Badger had already
gone into the village to get
supplies, so Ratty and he
were alone in Toad Hall.

As soon as Ratty had
left the room, Toad hopped
out of bed. First he tried the
door, but that was locked.
"No matter," he thought,
and he began to knot
together the sheets from
his bed to make a rope.

Then he put on his best
suit and filled his pockets
with all the money he could
find. Toad felt very pleased
with himself.

Smiling broadly, he tied
one end of the rope to the
window frame and began
scrambling down it as quickly
as he could.

When he reached the ground, Toad set off in the opposite direction to the village.

"I expect Ratty is still fetching the doctor," Toad said to himself, and he began to whistle a merry tune as he hopped and skipped along. "Poor Ratty! Of course, he meant well. They all did, but how could they imagine that the great and mighty Toad would stay a prisoner for long!"

Toad couldn't make up his mind where to go so he just kept on walking until he came to a little town.

Toad had worked up quite an appetite
from his long walk. He looked around for
somewhere to eat and marched into the first
inn that caught his eye.

By now he was sure that Badger and the
others would never catch up with him. He
sat down at the table near the counter and
ordered a very large and lavish meal.

Toad was already on his third sausage
when the driver of a smart and expensive-
looking motor car came in and began
talking about his car with the innkeeper.

Toad listened in to every word. He no longer felt hungry at all. He couldn't even finish the sausage for thinking about the car.

At last he got up and went outside to have a look at the motor car for himself. It was magnificent! It was everything a great car should be.

"I wonder if it starts easily?" he asked himself. "I expect it does!"

And before Toad knew what he was doing, he had taken hold of the starting handle and was turning it.

The car started like a dream and at the sound of the roaring engine Toad's eyes gleamed brightly.

In a flash he hopped into the driving seat, with one hand on the wheel, the other on the gear lever. Toad revved the engine and the car began to move, slowly at first and then it gathered speed.

As he sped along the country lanes Toad had never felt so happy, but it did not last for long. He drove the car so fast and so recklessly that soon the traffic police were after him. Silly, foolish Toad!

Before the morning was over, he had been arrested and brought before the judge.

"Dear me!" said the judge as Toad stood before him under the guard of a watchful policeman. "You have stolen a car and driven it dangerously through the countryside. And you have been cheeky to a policeman."

"Not guilty!" said Toad in a feeble voice.

"Nonsense!" said the judge. "There is no excuse for your crimes. You are guilty and you must go to prison. I sentence you to twenty years."

Toad was then placed in chains and taken from the courthouse to a nearby castle, struggling and protesting all the way. There he was thrown into the darkest dungeon.

"How can I ever hope to be free again?" he sobbed.

Even the daily visits by the jailer's daughter to bring him hot buttered toast did not cheer him up at first. But as the weeks passed, Toad told the girl all about the magnificent Toad Hall and she grew very fond of him.

And, of couse, she knew from Toad's boastful stories how rich he was. Her aunt was a washerwoman at the prison, and she also heard about Mr Toad's money.

One day, the girl said to Toad that she had a plan to get him out of prison.

Her plan was simple. For a few gold sovereigns, her aunt would bring some of her oldest washerwoman clothes and a bonnet, which Toad could wear to escape the prison in disguise.

Toad thought this was an excellent plan,
and agreed at once.

The very next Saturday, the jailer's
daughter brought her aunt to Toad's cell,
and together they dressed
him in the washer-
woman's old
clothes.

Then the girl tied
up her aunt to make it
look as though Toad
had overpowered her
to steal the clothes and
escape.

Toad rewarded them
both with gold coins as
promised, and stepped
out of the dungeon.

Clutching a bundle of washing, Toad made his way through the castle.

His heart was beating so fast he thought the guards must surely hear it. But he carried on, and every door and gate was opened for him.

It seemed like hours until, at last, he crossed the drawbridge that led out of the castle. Toad sighed with relief. He was free! All he could think about now was returning home.

24

Dizzy with the success
of his daring escape, Toad made for the
railway station. He pushed his way to the
head of the queue, and asked for a ticket to
the nearest village to Toad Hall.

But when he groped in the pocket of
his old apron for money, he was dismayed
to find that he had left it all behind in the
prison with the rest of his belongings.

"No money, no ticket," said the ticket
clerk. And Toad was pushed out of the way.

In despair, Toad wandered on to the platform and stared sadly up at the huge red engine waiting to depart.

"What's the matter, dear lady?" asked the kindly engine driver.

"I've l-lost all my money and I c-can't get home," stammered Toad, shedding a crocodile tear.

Thinking him a poor washer-woman, the engine driver took pity on Toad and offered to let him ride up on the footplate.

Soon the train was on its way.

As they passed through a wood, there came the roar of another engine close behind. "They're after me!" Toad thought. And when the engine slowed down at a bend, Toad jumped off and rolled down the slope.

Toad went on rolling down the grassy embankment until he came to rest against a tree. He could hardly believe his luck as the pursuing engine thundered past.

It was crowded with policemen and soldiers. "I've outwitted them all!" he chuckled, highly pleased with himself. "What a smart fellow I am!"

After he made sure he had no broken bones, Toad made his way deeper into the woods. He was both hungry and tired, but the thought of his own cleverness kept him in good spirits.

Toad kept on walking until it grew dark
and then, at last, tired out, he found shelter
in the hollow of a tree. He closed his eyes
and was soon fast asleep.

That night Toad had no bad dreams.
Instead he dreamt he was safely back at
Toad Hall being given a hero's welcome by
all his friends.